MARIGOLD CYANIDE

AGNIBHA SENGUPTA

INDIA • SINGAPORE • MALAYSIA

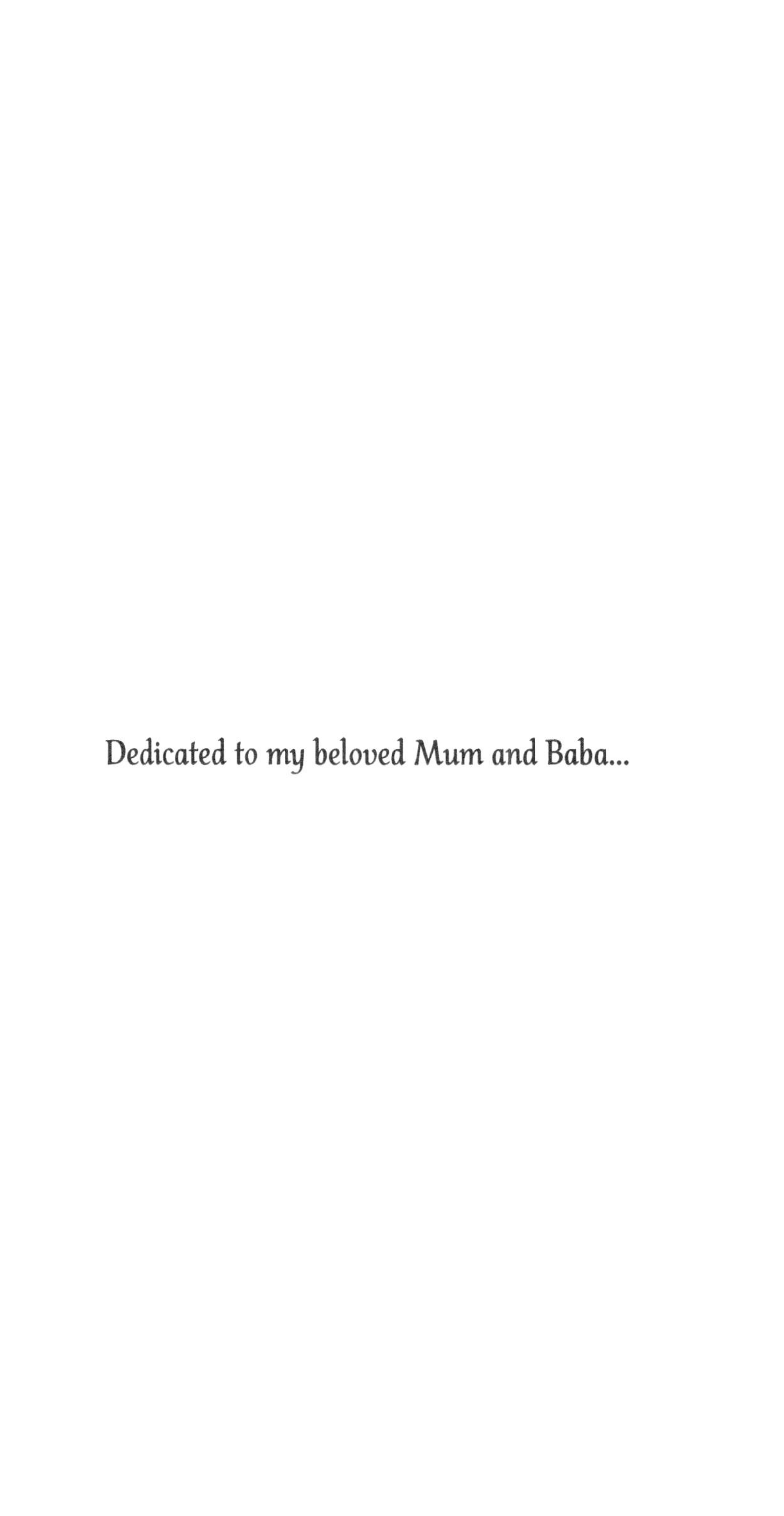

Dedicated to my beloved Mum and Baba...

CONTENTS

CONTENTS

ACKNOWLEDGEMENTS

Bringing **Marigold Cyanide** to life has been a journey filled with discovery, challenge, and immense growth. I would like to express my deepest gratitude to everyone who stood by me throughout this adventure.

To my family, for your unwavering encouragement and faith in my dreams, even on the days when I doubted myself. Your love and support have been my anchor.

To my friends and neighbours, who patiently listened to my ideas, offered thoughtful feedback, and motivated me to keep going when the road felt long.

To my respected teachers from school, who have encouraged me on my path. Your unwavering support has been like a true pillar to a monument, helping me build the foundation of my dreams.

A special thanks to Jyotsna Mam, and Notion Press team for your guidance and expertise, which helped refine this story and bring it to its full potential.

Finally, to my readers—thank you for picking up this book and embarking on this mystery with Sen. Your curiosity and enthusiasm make storytelling the greatest adventure of all.

This book is as much yours as it is mine.

AUTHOR'S NOTE

Writing Marigold Cyanide has been a fulfilling and enriching experience for me. The story had begun with my love for mysteries, and a simple yet sinister connection between human emotions and crime. As the plot grew, so did my passion for creating a tale that was not only suspenseful but also deeply personal.

Through this novel, I have explored dark themes of trust, betrayal, and the lengths to which people can go to protect their secrets. I hope that as you turn the pages, you'll find yourself immersed in the mystery and feel the same curiosity and excitement that guided me as I wrote it.

I'd like to take a moment to thank you, the reader, for picking up this book. Your willingness to embark on this journey with me means the world. I hope

Marigold Cyanide leaves you questioning every clue and savouring every twist until the very end.

Cheers! And, Happy Sleuthing!

Warm regards,

Agnibha Sengupta (Your Beloved Author).

Class X, Vivekananda Mission School, Joka

Chapter 1

THE PALASHBARI ESTATE

As the fog settled in on the murky afternoon, the city of joy awaited the impending rainfall expected later in the evening. Peering out from the windows, residents observed the brooding sky, its overcast demeanor evoking a sense of mystery for some and a familiar calm for others. A curious mind always wanders about strangeness. The house had always seemed peculiar. A large mansion. The sprawling estate of Palashbari, gleamed against the clouds. It was owned by some wealthy man, Haricharan Raychaudhuri. However, the family had issues... Issues which cannot be explained by natural causes.

Two murders have been haunting the halls of Palashbari estate. One- the murder of Haricharan's wife; Second- the murder of the daughter of Haricharan. The factor which prowls these murders is their style of execution- each victim was found holding a cyanide-laced marigold...

Formerly revered as a harbinger of peace, the marigold now conceals its deadly intent, morphing into an unsuspected weapon in the shadows...

On that fateful afternoon, Haricharan sat at his desk engrossed in the scrutiny of critical documents, their significance palpable in the air. Two sealed letters, their crimson wax seals juxtaposed against weathered parchment, lay conspicuously at the edge of his workspace. Ignoring the rumbling thunder outside, Haricharan delved deeper into his task. Abruptly, a sizable paper wad struck him with force, sending him reeling in shock as he collapsed to the ground. With adrenaline coursing through his veins, he bolted towards the window, hoping to catch a glimpse of the assailant. But the fleeting shadow vanished into the ether, leaving Haricharan grasping at thin air, his pursuit futile...

Haricharan unfolded the crumpled piece of paper. Reading the contents written on it, his veins surged a mix of shock and apprehension. Paralyzed by terror, he remained frozen, his eyes fixated on the ominous words scrawled across the crumpled paper. Because, on it were the words:

"Beware,

You are under strict vigil...

Any wrong move will cost you,

And, you will be awarded with the prize- of DEATH..."

Tossing the paper aside, he hastily donned his coat, clutching the letters and the crumpled paper ball tightly. With determination etched on his face, he departed for an undisclosed destination, leaving his family members to grapple with the palpable fear that radiated from him, a fear too profound to be articulated in mere words.

Chapter 2

A STRANGER

It was another house along Park Street, just past the famous Peter Cat. Taking the right turn down the narrow gully, the house emerged—old, yet dignified, much like the man who occupied it. The evening air was heavy, and inside, a silhouette hovered by the window. As the figure came into focus, it revealed a young man, no older than twenty-five or twenty-six, his unruly curls framing a face untouched by a comb. Thin-framed glasses perched on his nose, their rounded lenses magnifying the intensity of his gaze. He held a cup of coffee, taking a slow sip before sighing softly.

"Let him in," he murmured, barely louder than the ticking clock behind him.

At his command, the servant opened the door, revealing **Haricharan Raychaudhuri**. The older man hesitated for a moment before stepping inside, his gaze shifting around the modest room. Without a word, he settled into the chair indicated by the young detective, whose expression remained inscrutable.

"I've come to seek your help, Mr. Sen," Haricharan finally spoke, his voice edged with unease.

Sen set his cup down carefully and met his guest's eyes. "You needn't call me 'Mr.' I'm much younger."

Haricharan nodded, visibly uncomfortable. "I believe I am in danger," he continued, his voice lowering as though the words themselves might draw unwanted attention.

"For that, I'll need to know who you are," Sen replied calmly, gesturing for more details.

Haricharan drew in a breath. "Haricharan Raychaudhuri."

Sen leaned back slightly, studying the man before him. He recognized the name. "And what is it that stalks you?"

Haricharan fumbled in his coat pocket, pulling out a set of crumpled letters, his hands trembling as he passed them over. "These threats... They've been arriving for weeks."

Sen unfolded each letter with deliberate care, his eyes scanning the cryptic messages. "I'll keep these for my investigation?"

"S-Sure," Haricharan stammered, wiping his brow.

Sen glanced back at him. "This could be a prank. Have you thought of that?"

Haricharan shook his head, his voice growing tense. "It's not a prank. I own the Palashbari estate. It's a huge mansion... you must have heard of the Raychaudhuri family."

Sen raised an eyebrow. "I'm familiar."

"Our family has had rivals for generations. These threats... I believe they're a warning. My son has been missing for years, and I've kept the property in his name through the will. But now... after my wife and daughter were murdered, I fear I am next."

Sen's eyes narrowed. "You mentioned two murders? How were they committed?"

Haricharan swallowed hard, his voice dropping to a near whisper. "Both victims were found with a marigold in hand. Forensic reports confirmed... cyanide-laced."

Sen leaned forward, intrigued. "A marigold?"

Haricharan nodded gravely. "We have a garden in the estate. But the only flower that grows there... is the marigold."

Sen remained silent for a moment, his mind already piecing together the facts. "I'll help you," he said finally, his voice low but firm. "Tomorrow morning, I'll visit your estate. This case—oddly interesting—might be one of the strangest I've encountered."

Haricharan handed Sen the address of Palashbari estate, his relief palpable as he rose from the chair. Without another word, he departed, leaving Sen alone with the ominous letters.

Sen glanced at the crumpled papers one last time before muttering under his breath, "A marigold as a lethal weapon... this case will defy the laws of crime."

Chapter 3

CHARISMATIC SEN

It had all started with the letter. Sen was called on for a case. He proved his worth, as a sleuth. Cracking open the case of a mystique pearl, which was followed by the untimely demise of its host. Sen, accepts it to be his fault. He could never return after that 'accident'...

Sen shifted from London, to his home town, Kolkata. Sen, decided to reside at a home near Park Street, Kolkata. At an amateur age of 25, he already had cases up his sleeve. Cases which could make him think all day long.

Sen had started spending his days in this profession. Solving the smallest of cases, theft, robbery, etc. Suddenly, he heard about the confusing 'death' of his neighbor. Sen was appointed for investigation. The body of his neighbor could not be found. The police were hopeless, and had done everything in their power. It was up to Sen, to solve this ridiculous case, which seemed so obvious. Obvious, as described by the policemen. On searching the room, with the guidance of Sen, they found a diary tucked in the bed covers. Sen took it, and started skimming through it. He found, that his neighbor had written his diary, on the day of his possible 'death'. The servants, told Sen that, Mr. Kishore (Sen's neighbor) had gone out for a walk. The time was 3pm in the afternoon. In the fresh sun, Kishore had given an excuse of meeting someone important.

After, a difficult inquiry, Mr. Kishore was found in a warehouse, tied up, and shut with tape. He had bruises all over, and was bleeding. On rescue, he was immediately taken to hospital. The doctors confirmed that Mr. Kishore had been in that state for 6 days for the light wound near his head had partially healed.

Sen came to the conclusion. On that day, everyone known to Mr. Kishore was called for the final testament. Sen, started. He explained everything in detail. The case which was abandoned by the police, was getting enlightened by Sen with mere words. Words, which were true in all senses. He had proven everything. How, Mr. Kishore's most trusted friend, Mr. Sainath, had held Mr. Kishore hostage. Kishore and Sainath were in argument. Both of them worked in the same company, where Mr. Kishore was the boss. Sainath could not accept this, and decided to eliminate Kishore. He started insulting Kishore, and went into arguments, which were violent at times. All relations were shattered between them. Kishore, wanted to calm Sainath down. Thus, he went out on that afternoon to meet Sainath on the bridge, and then everyone knew what happened.

Sainath rose, and became aggressive, "How dare you? You futile detective? How will you prove your worthless words? HUH!?"

Sen replied gently, "Sir, you might want to sit back down, because I have all of the proof, the police need to get you in the Jail."

"WHAT PR-PROOF?"

"The place where you had captured Mr. Kishore, had a small tea-stall. Upon questioning the owner, I have come to know, that Mr. Kishore had bought a cup of tea on that day, and went ahead to be held captive... If you want more proof, I have all of it ready. But I think you wouldn't want that, would you?"

Sainath, dropped and hid his head between his arms.

"I-I-I's sorry..."

The police went ahead, and dragged Sainath up. Sainath was taken to the Jail, sentenced to 5 years. Later, it was heard that Sainath committed suicide...

Chapter 4

ARRIVAL OF DETECTIVE SEN

Sen has now become a renowned detective in town, after he made the solution to the intrigue-rising case of his missing neighbor. All headlines spoke about him, and from then he has been solving cases. But, a case of this big reputation, and kind has never approached Sen.

Sen, has been popularly referred to as Detective Sen for no one knows his first name. Detective Sen's idea of a crime is different from others. He believes in simplicity being the art of murder. However, killing a person with a cyanide-laced marigold seems unexpected. And, so it does to everyone in the Palashbari estate.

Sen went to make a call to his driver downstairs. The car was booked to arrive the next morning.

Sen went back upstairs, and leaned back on his easy chair. His mind revolved around this shocking case.

Chapter 5

THE MURDER

Haricharan usually stays up till late of night, to finish his work. He was doing the same this night, although fear preyed upon him. He had his lights on. Everyone was asleep in the house. Except Haricharan. His eyes were coming to a stop. He wanted to go to sleep. From nowhere, he heard footsteps outside his room. He looked back, but no one was there. A sinister-figure wearing a mask, as it seemed so in the limelight, started approaching Haricharan with soft footsteps. Haricharan was already sleepy, so he paid no attention to it. He started to drool, when the mysterious figure grabbed him by the mouth.

Haricharan struggled, unable to word himself. He tried to break free. The enigmatic figure held something near the nose of Haricharan, which made him immediately tumble. He lied on the ground.

The figure made Haricharan hold something in his hand. And, walked out.

Haricharan lied cold on the floor. In his hands were held a sank marigold. The threat came to be true. Haricharan was awarded with the prize of death...

Chapter 6

AFTERMATH

Sen woke up next morning to the sound of his doorbell. The newspapers were being delivered. He opened the door and took the newspaper, to keep on the table. His servant arrived with Sen's morning cup of coffee. Sen freshened himself up, and went to read the news. On the front page, was a headline which shocked Sen to his arteries. He felt defeated, and punched his hand on the table. "Why hadn't I?", murmured Sen. Sen rushed downstairs, and asked for his driver to arrive at the instant. The newspaper lay on the floor... The headlines read,

"The owner of the famous Palashbari estate, Haricharan Raychaudhuri found dead in his room. A marigold held in his hand..."

Chapter 7

THE CRIME SCENE

Sen took his coat with him, and wore it in the car. He gave his driver the address of Palashbari estate given by Haricharan. "Fast, fast...", demanded Sen. Sen wiped sweat from his forehead. After a ride of about 30-45 minutes, Sen arrived at Palashbari estate. The gate was huge, made of pure steel, but stained. The mansion looked like a fortress of the Raychaudhuri family. The walls were a dimmed cream. The grass looked greener on the other side. The garden came in Sen's notice. The marigolds were in bloom. Spring was starting to spread its colors. Sen, 'beat the doorbell', as it seemed so as there was no 'doorbell', but a large handle which had to be pounded onto the steel. Metals produce a sonorous effect.

A tall, nut-brown, man wearing a white pajama and a blue shirt, approached the gate.

"Who are you?", asked the man.

"I am Sen. Detective Sen. Mr. Haricharan had come up to me yesterday"

"Oh! You are the detective; dada was talking about. Come in."

Sen entered the opened gate, and looked around. Nobody was there to be seen. The man who had enquired Sen, closed the gate and escorted Sen till the Darbar, or the living room.

Sen asked, "Who are you from the family?"

"I am not of the family dada. I am their house worker who has been staying with them for ages since. They treat me as a family member..."

"Hmm..."

Sen was shown into a narrow hall. He was instructed to walk straight through the hall. The house worker bid goodbye, and went back. Sen followed the instructions, and walked straight. Eventually, he reached the Darbar (the meeting room). All family members were gathered in the living room. Everyone looked up at Sen with nasty glances. One of them adjusted their glasses, and inquired, "Now, who might you be?"

"I am Sen. Detective Sen. Mr. Haricharan had accosted me to investigate the cause of death if he will be murdered, which I suspect he has been. And, I have seen in the news that he already is dead. In the same manner, two murders have occurred in your past."

"Who told you all this? Dada?"

"Yes, your dada, Mr. Haricharan"

"Fine then, what do you want us all to do? Act like your puppets for two weeks?"

"I may not fit the mold of a traditional detective as you might expect. But rest assured, the truth that spills from my lips has a way of piercing through even the most fortified criminal minds."

The man stopped speaking.

Sen continued, "If you all would introduce yourselves, it will be easier for me to address..."

The man who was speaking earlier with Sen, said, "I am the cousin of Haricharan, Ramesh Raychaudhuri"

Ramesh pointed at two old people sitting in the corner, with their heads down in regret, as it looked so in the detective's eye; and said, "Those are my parents, Mr. Preetimohan Raychaudhuri and Mrs. Hemlata Raychaudhuri.".

Ramesh, then pointed towards another stranger standing beside the parents of Haricharan, and said, "That is my dada's secretary, Mr. Amit Patel."

"Very good!", exclaimed Sen giving a sharp look at everyone.

Sen continued, "I shall come back tomorrow and go on with the interrogation. By the way, Mr. Ramesh, please keep them ready tomorrow morning for my debriefing. Thank you..."

Sen walked out of the living room. All had questions in mind including Sen. Amidst all questions, was one answer. And, that answer is what Sen will have to decipher.

Chapter 8

LINGERING DOUBT

Sen went back to the gate. Something struck him. He looked at the garden. He wanted to draw near to it, but his urge could not be satisfied. Sen, re-entered his car, and went back to his home at Russell Street. Sen, had already called for the car to come next morning.

Sen held his revolver, and thought to himself. Will he need it?

He always carries his notebook with him.

Sen waited till next morning. He leaned back on his easy chair. His mind was filled with considerations. Who is the serial murderer, who has challenged the wits of Detective Sen? Sleep did not come to Sen... The answer remained unknown...

Chapter 9

MEANWHILE...

Meanwhile, at Palashbari estate. Everything was going wrong. The dinner was set on the table. Everyone came to have their usual dinner. However, it did not end up as 'usual', and one of them raised the doubt of Haricharan's murder and the arrival of a detective. One of them flapped their hands on the table, and spoke, "Enough of this 'will'-ly business. All of you please shut up. Whatever fate was written in the name of Hari, has been delivered to him!"

And, so it was. It was quiet, as no one talked to each other for the rest of the night. And, for many more nights to come...

Chapter 10

EVIL BEGINS...

Sen woke up to the sound of his car's honk. He quickly brushed, and had a shower. Then, rushed out of the house like Usain Bolt, to hop into the car. He instructed the driver, "Take me to Palashbari estate. The one which I visited yesterday. Fast, Kumar, fast!"

So, the car swiftly dashed on the road towards Palashbari estate, like a gust of wind on a cold morning.

The car came to an abrupt stop in front of the straggling estate of Palashbari. Ramesh Raychaudhuri was already waiting for Sen at the gate. He welcomed Sen, without a smile. Sen folded his hands. Ramesh showed Sen the way into the Darbar again, and asked, "Will you have breakfast with us?"

"No... Thanks"

There was the grand table in the large dining hall. Breakfast for the family was laid out on the same. The inside of the dining hall was royal. A chandelier hung from the roof, spreading the light onto the entire hall. Sen felt like a 'Raychaudhuri' in the mansion.

Sen asked, "Have you prepared everyone for the interrogation, Mr. Ramesh?"

"Yes, Sen. I have…"

"Quite so… Now, where should I go?"

Ramesh instructed him to go to the Darbar for the questioning session. Ramesh will be responsible for sending each individual. Sen murmured, "Very good…"

Sen took a seat on the couch, and looked up at the corridor. Coming near to him was a shadow, which looked of an old man. The shadow drew nearer every instant…

Chapter 11

MR. PREETIMOHAN RAYCHAUDHURI

In front of Sen, came Mr. Preetimohan Raychaudhuri, father of Ramesh and Haricharan Raychaudhuri. Sen asked him to be seated. Mr. Preetimohan stationed himself in front of Sen, on an imperial chair. He was old, and had white hair. He had a clean-shaved beard, and an uneven moustache. He was wearing very usual clothes. A yellow sherwani with a white dhoti. Sen started by asking, "You must be Mr. Preetimohan Raychaudhuri?"

"Hm!"

"Your sons are- Haricharan Raychaudhuri and Ramesh Raychaudhuri?"

"Yes."

"Well, I hope you realize the untimely demise of your son, Mr. Haricharan Raychaudhuri?"

"Yes."

"Very well, who is older- Mr. Haricharan or Mr. Ramesh?"

"Haricharan."

"Why was property transferred only to Mr. Haricharan?"

"He was older and much more responsible than his you-younger brother."

"Hm! Mr. Haricharan's son is missing, isn't is so?"

"Yes. He has been missing for several years now."

"Who had the property entitled by Mr. Haricharan?"

"His son."

"Why?"

"How am I supposed to know that?"

"Hm! Why hadn't his daughter got a part of share?"

"Family traditions."

"What is the family tradition?"

"Only males get the share of property."

"Mr. Haricharan had transferred property to his son, but his son was missing. Why?"

"Maybe, he expected his son to return someday."

"Very well. That should be it from your side..."

Mr. Preetimohan got up, and folded his hands. He turned and walked down the hallway. His shadow slowly disappeared from view.

Chapter 12

MRS. HEMLATA RAYCHAUDHURI

Sen called, "Next!"

Another silhouette gradually came near towards Sen. It was of a female. The figure finally came into light. It was Mrs. Hemlata Raychaudhuri, wife of Mr. Preetimohan and mother of Ramesh and Haricharan Raychaudhuri. She looked as simple as Mr. Preetimohan. She had white hair as well, and was wearing glasses of high quality. She was wearing a long-drawn pale red saree. Sen asked her, to take a seat. Mrs. Hemlata settled herself on the same chair, in front of Sen. Sen queried, "You must be the wife of Mr. Preetimohan Raychaudhuri?"

"Hm!"

"You had two sons- Mr. Haricharan and Mr. Ramesh Raychaudhuri?"

"Yes."

"Well, did you ever object towards Mr. Haricharan inheriting the property? And, not Mr. Ramesh?"

"Haricharan was much more responsible in our senses."

"Did Mr. Haricharan reject his inheritance?"

"No."

"How many years has Mr. Haricharan's son been missing?"

"Several. I think seventeen years."

"How old are you and your husband?"

"Around 90"

"Why did Mr. Preetimohan transfer all property to Mr. Haricharan, even though he is alive?"

"He is already not well. While having caught up with a heart disease at 75 years, how would he control the estate? Thus..."

"Is there any other reason?"

"Cultural and traditional beliefs."

"Like?"

"The Raychaudhuri family has been exchanging property for decades now. It has always been done when the former owner was alive."

"Very well. You can go…"

"Thank you so much…", saying this Mrs. Hemlata got up and dissociated into the dim hallway. Another contour of someone was coming closer to the Darbar. It grew bigger by time…

Chapter 13

MR. AMIT PATEL

In front of Sen came, the exhausted Mr. Amit Patel, secretary of Mr. Haricharan Raychaudhuri. Mr. Amit placed himself on the same chair in front of Sen. He was a normal man, suitable for the post of secretary. The scent of his perfume smeared all across the room. Sen asked, "You are Mr. Amit Patel, secretary of the deceased, Mr. Haricharan?"

"Hmm..."

"Well. Had you observed any changes in Mr. Haricharan recently?"

"Yes. He seemed worried all the time."

"Could you figure out any possible reason for that? Or, did he ever tell you anything?"

"I had asked once. He answered me, and said that it was his will that was worrying him. Whether he had done the right thing or not by giving his share of property to his son, and not his daughter before his daughter's unfortunate death. His son was also missing for years. He also showed me some letters, which were probably threats, as he said so."

"Very well. Was Mr. Haricharan a happy person?"

"Of course. I have not seen a jollier person than him."

"Who was the lawyer of Mr. Haricharan?"

"Senior advocate, Rakesh Bhuiyan"

"Good. You shall go now. Please send in the house worker of the family next."

Mr. Amit got up, and walked into the vague hallway. In, walked another person. Another person to interrogate...

Chapter 14

PRAFULLA GHOSH

The same nut-brown man, met by Sen yesterday, walked in, and took a seat in front of Sen. He looked aged. He had wrinkles on his mouth. He was wearing glasses. He had a white cloth and dhoti on his body. Sen started yet again,

"What is your name?"

"Babu, Prafulla Ghosh."

"Hmm... How many years have you been working here?"

"Babu, I am here for 10 years. Oldest person in the work."

"Very well. Had you noticed any observable changes in Mr. Haricharan?"

"Dada, always seemed to be in tension. I have not been able to guess the reason."

"Had you ever seen Mr. Haricharan's son?"

"I have seen him being born. Then, after 2 years, dada announced that his son was missing..."

"You may go, Prafulla. If required, I shall call you again. Please call Mr. Ramesh once you leave the hall"

"Sure babu..."

Prafulla disappeared into the hallway. Another shade of black could be seen approaching Sen by the instant. It was another person. One last, person to interrogate...

Chapter 15

RAMESH RAYCHAUDHURI

Ramesh Raychaudhuri entered the room. He was a tall man, wearing glasses. He looked young despite his age. Being the cousin of Haricharan, he looked adolescent. He was wearing an orange shirt, with brown pajamas. Sen began, "You are Mr. Ramesh Raychaudhuri?"

"Yes."

"Did you ever feel betrayed, not having a share of property"

"Never."

"Why?"

"Dada, was always nice to me, and he even mentioned me in his will."

"How?"

"If his son does not actually show up, then it will be me, who shall inherit property."

"Why had your dada done this?"

"He loved me."

"Very well... Now, tell me, are you married?"

"No."

"Do you have any interests in flowers?"

"No."

"Didn't you object to Mr. Haricharan's son getting all the property?"

"N-no... Why would I? It was dada's family, and he had the right to do whatsoever."

"Good. You may go now... I want to inspect the garden. I suppose, I'm allowed to do so?"

"Sure... You can go *ahead.*"

Both Sen, and Ramesh Raychaudhuri rose. Ramesh walked down the hallway, and disappeared. Sen, made his way out of the mansion. The mansion really was old. It had worn off walls. The colors of the mansion were fading away. Half of the windows were shattered. Specially, Haricharan's...

Sen went ahead to examine the garden. Most of the garden was engrossed in marigolds. Sen looked ahead to check the marigolds. Suddenly, a metallic object struck Sen's foot. Sen, shifted his eyes, and picked up the object. It was a ring. The ring was made of gold, and had the letters, R.R., inscribed onto it. Sen, could make no meaning of it. He kept it in his pocket, and continued the investigation. Nothing more was found. Sen went ahead, and asked Ramesh whether he could leave. Sen left, and his car sped away towards his house. Sen, ran upstairs. He put down his coat, and placed the ring on his table. He looked at it carefully.

"Must... belong to the criminal.", spoke Sen.

The ring was shining as if new...

Chapter 16
UNKNOWN THREAT

After enquiring about certain things, Sen returned back to his house at Park Street. His servant opened the door, and let him in. Upon entering, Sen was confronted by a man who came rushing down the stairs. The unknown man, held Sen by his collar, and spat out, "DON'T YOU DARE! HARICHARAN DIED DUE TO HIS MISTAKES... NO ONE IS RESPONSIBL' FOR THAT SCOUNDREL's DEATH! THERE IS NOTHING TO INVESTIGATE ABOUT THIS MATTER!?"

"Well, Sir... I suppose Mr. Haricharan had been murdered. He was holding a marigold, which if examined would be found cyanide-laced. So..."

The man let go of Sen, and growled, "EYES ARE WHAT YOU WILL BE UNDER". Saying this, the stranger stormed out of the house banging the door behind him.

His final words were, "ALL OF THIS IS BALDERDASH!"

Sen went upstairs, and found a rolled-up letter on the table. Sen paid no heed to it, and kept the discovered ring beside the letter. He ordered for a cup of cappuccino. Sen leaned back on his easy-chair, and opened the letter. "Just as I had expected", muttered Sen.

The cappuccino was served, and he took a sip to relax himself. On the letter was, *"There is nothing for you to investigate...*

Haricharan has died, and it has nothing to do with you.

You will be under constant surveillance...

Wrong moves will be costly,

A cost, you will not be able to pay..."

Sen folded it neatly, and kept it where it was placed originally. Sen steepled, and thought about the unknown man's appearance. He could not observe it much. The person was wearing black trousers, and had a black mask on. He was wrapped around with a grey shawl. His hands were strong, for Sen's neck had started paining. Sen, wondered. Only if he could see the person's eyes, it would have been clearer. The stranger was wearing sneakers of the gradient, black and white. The outsider also had a ring on him, for Sen received a cut on his neck when the violent man let go of him. Sen was gradually understanding the gravity of the case. This investigation will be not be easy as it seems. Sen, has found himself already entangled in the web of enigma. In a web, from where it is hard to escape without answers...

Chapter 17

AN OLD ACCOMPLICE

The next morning came. Sen, rushed downstairs and towards the police station. He was greeted with warmth from his well-known officer, Mr. Prasad.

"Sen, is it? Come, come... Have a seat. What is the matter?"

Sen took a seat, and a breather. He explained the Palashbari affair to Prasad. The officer listened attentively, and at certain intervals nodded and murmured, "Hm!".

Sen finished his account, and paused. Prasad asked,

"How will I be able to help you in this case?"

"I need some search warrants, and you by my side, Mr. Prasad. Please."

"I can try... But be careful Sen. The Palashbari estate is a very renowned family in Kolkata."

"I know. That's why I need your help to organize things."

"But you are quite a good sleuth!"

"I am new to this..."

"Aight' when are you taking me for investigation?"

"That's the spirit. You can pick me up at around 12 p.m. from my home. We shall head straight to the next set of suspects!"

"And, who are they supposedly?"

"The business rivals of Palashbari estate- Shyamlal & Sons. Along with Kumar Enterprises."

"Sure... Meet you at 12"

Sen rose, and bid goodbye.

Sen could hear a few words from the officers, sitting at their desks, when he was leaving. They were all saying,

"A strange fellow... He is, is he not?"

Sen turned back, smiled and replied, "Ain't I?"

Chapter 18

SHYAMLAL & SONS

The clock had hit 12. Prasad came to meet Sen. He found Sen sitting, and thinking with his eyes closed. Prasad interrupted, "Sen... It's time... Let's go."

Sen opened his eyes, and looked at prasad. He pleaded Prasad to lead the way till the car. Sen got up, and wore his coat. The car was waiting right outside the door. Sen went in, and sat down. Prasad occupied the front seat, and asked, "So where exactly is this Shyamlal and Sons.?"

"Bagbazaar, Chaurasi Street, beside the Pal Medicine Shop."

Prasad instructed the driver about the same, and the car started gaining speed. Sen closed his eyes again, and went into deep thought.

Prasad again said, "Didn't get much sleep Sen, is it?"

Sen did not answer, only nodded slowly...

It was almost 12:30 when they arrived at their destined location. The Shyamlal and Sons.

The shop looked quite old. The letters on the signboard had lost their shine. The door was made of wood, which had started worsening. But it could be well understood that the shop made a lot of income from their business of textile. Sen entered the shop, and looked around at the well-decorated interior. Sen was asked by a woman, "What do you need Sir?"

'I need the manager. Mr. Harshit Shyamlal."

"Surely Sir, please come this way."

Sen told Prasad to lead the way, and Sen stayed behind, observing everything to the fullest.

Eventually after a flight of stairs, came the glass door. The door was opened and, Sen entered.

The woman said to the accoutered, seated man, "Sir, they have come to meet you."

The old man said in a grumpy voice, "Who are you folks?"

"We are from the police.", Sen answered, and gestured the woman to leave.

The old man continued, "What proof do you have for that?"

Sen reached out to his pocket, and took out a wallet. He pulled a card out of it, and handed it to the old man.

"Mr. Sen... Detective?", asked the old man.

"Yes."

"Namaskar. I am Mr. Harshit Shyamlal. The owner of the Shyamlal & Sons. What brings you folk here?"

"We shall ask you certain questions."

"What for?"

"The owner of Haricharan Enterprise, Mr. Haricharan Raychaudhuri has been found dead yesterday. We suspect it to be a murder."

Shyamlal wiped some sweat, and nodded.

"It is a sad matter. What more can he do?"

"Your company had bad relations with him, am I not, right?"

"Competition is always there between two companies. Specially, when both produce and run for the same thing. Haricharan's company always wished for our downfall, but we never wished for theirs! Never did we."

"Can I assume? That, you might be counted as an enemy?"

"IF you want to, you can. I have no obstruction. You have to do your own work. But I can safely tell one thing. Even if our competition was rigid, I would never kill my opposition. Never would I!"

The old man slammed his hand on the table, and folded his hands.

Sen looked at the man, exchanged glances, and folded his hands in return.

Prasad asked, "Sen, how do you find this Shyamlal?"

"Very mysterious, Mr. Prasad. Very mysterious."

Sen walked out of the shop, and bought a packet of gum from the medicine shop. He asked the shopkeeper,

"Do you know who Mr. Haricharan is?"

"Yes babu. He is a Raychaudhuri of our city. Unfortunate demise... Very unfortunate."

"Can you tell me where is, Kumar Enterprises?"

"Yes babu. You have to go straight from here to Gariahat. There, beside the book shop, is Kumar Enterprises."

"Had Mr. Haricharan ever come here?"

"I don't think so Babu. My work is to take care of my medicine shop, I have not quite paid attention to anyone entering the Shyamlal & Sons. But I remember once. Yes, once Mr. Haricharan had bought a pair of tablets for blood pressure from me. I don't remember when."

"Thank you. Thank you so much..."

Sen went in the car. Prasad paid the shopkeeper, and got himself seated. The next destination was told to their driver. And, the car drifted off.

Sen kept his eyes open, and perceived the various scenes which went by. Somehow, his face looked positive. It was as though; he was able to solve some complications from his end.

But this is just the beginning...

Chapter 19

KUMAR ENTERPRISES

Gariahat arrived. The lane beside the book store was followed, and Sen arrived in front of the Kumar Enterprises. It was also an old shop, which had undergone some renovation in the past.

Sen murmured, "Let's go in... Come Mr. Prasad."

Prasad accompanied Sen till the gate. The guards stopped Sen, and asked, "What need?"

"I have to meet the owner, Mr. Rakshit Kumar."

"Why so?"

"We are from the police, investigating a murder."

"Sir is busy."

"We don't care. Where does he sit?"

"Go inside, and take left down the stairs, to the room."

Sen nodded, and pushed the door open. He stormed past the people, and down the stairs."

There was the door to the room, which was partially open. Sen didn't even knock, and opened the door. Mr. Rakshit, looked at Sen suspiciously, and told on his phone, "Hmm... I'll call you back after few time"

The call was hung, and Sen exchanged glances. Mr. Rakshit spat out,

"HOW Dare you!? Enter my room, and disturb my call! Raju! Where is this, Raju?"

Sen snapped the other's speech, and said,

"Your secretary has been outside. We have told him who we are, and now you shall know."

Sen folded his hands, and continued,

"I am Sen. Detective Sen. He is Mr. Prasad, commissioner of the police. We are here investigating the murder of Mr. Haricharan..."

"Hmm... What about it folks? I don't care what happens to that Haricharan."

"You hated him, that means?"

"If you place it like that, then that's that..."

"Why is that so?"

"He was a scoundrel. How he treated us! We had gone to his damned company for some assistance... He shooed us away like animals. It's good, he's dead."

"Those words do not seem right, Mr. Rakshit. This means, you had a motive to kill Mr. Haricharan?"

"Yes. I had the motive. I always wanted to remove him. But it is my arthritis which holds me. And, my fear of the sight of blood."

"Then, Mr. Rakshit, I must say, Mr. Haricharan was not killed by stabbing."

"What!?"

"Yes. Mr. Rakshit, he was killed with cyanide. I can't count you out."

Sen rose, and folded his hands. He left, with Mr. Prasad hurdling behind him. Mr. Rakshit Kumar was white with fear. He sat cold in his place not moving. His phone was ringing...

Prasad asked Sen, "How did you find Mr. Rakshit?"

"Not guilty of murder."

"But he just told you he had an excellent motive for murder. Did you really believe his arthritis story?"

"It was not a story."

"Why do you say so?"

"I saw tablets for treating arthritis on his table, under a pile of books."

"Well, if you have seen so, we have to believe you."

Sen opened the door of the car, and went in. Prasad accompanied the front seat, and instructed the driver to go back at Sen's. He asked Sen,

"What is your next plan?"

"To converse with the Raychaudhuris"

"You told you have done so."

"I believe they all are lying. All of them have a motive to kill Mr. Haricharan. I need to dig out those secrets from them."

"Well, we can do it tomorrow. For now, take some rest. And for the forensics that you asked for, the marigolds were cyanide-laced as you said..."

The car arrived at Sen's mansion. Sen rose, and knocked on his door. His servant opened the same. Sen waved his hand at Prasad, and the car drove away. Sen entered the house, and asked for a cup of tea. He rushed upstairs, and seated himself on his easy-chair. He took the letter of threat, and read it again, and again...

Finally, he murmured, "Cleanly typed..."

Chapter 20

CONVERSING WITH THE RAYCHAUDHURIS

Dawn had broken early that day. Sen rushed to the Palashabari estate for his second interrogation, which might be his last. All alone. No police. Only Sen, and the Raychaudhuris.

Sen ticked off the first name in his notebook- Mr. Preetimohan Raychaudhuri.

The room was heavy with the scent of old wood and dust, the air thick with the weight of secrets long buried. Mr. Preetimohan sat opposite Sen, his back straight in the plush chair, his hands resting calmly on his lap. For a man who had just lost his son, Preetimohan was oddly composed, his face betraying no emotion.

Sen studied the old man carefully for the second time, noting the subtle movements—the way his fingers occasionally flexed, the slight tilt of his head when he spoke, the unreadable gleam in his eyes. Sen had obtained new eyes.

"Mr. Preetimohan," Sen began, his voice soft but probing. "You've lost your eldest son. And yet, you don't seem... affected."

Preetimohan's eyes flickered, but only for a moment. "Grief comes in many forms, Detective. I've lived long enough to know that life moves on. Haricharan was... a complicated man."

Sen raised an eyebrow, leaning slightly forward. "Complicated how?"

Preetimohan smiled, but there was no warmth in it. "You knew Haricharan. Ambitious, stubborn, always thinking he was above the rest of us. But in the end, it seems even he wasn't above death."

There was something in the way Preetimohan said it—too detached, too rehearsed. Sen let the silence stretch, watching as Preetimohan's hands moved to adjust the cufflinks on his shirt, small gold pieces that gleamed faintly in the dim light.

"You didn't agree with Haricharan inheriting the estate, did you?" Sen pressed.

Preetimohan's eyes narrowed, just slightly. "He was the eldest. It was tradition. What I thought didn't matter."

"And yet, he bypassed you, didn't he? Passed the estate directly to his son, despite your position as the patriarch of the family."

Preetimohan's hands stilled. The silence grew heavier. "Tradition holds its own power, Detective. What's done is done."

Sen caught the briefest flicker of something—anger, perhaps, or regret. He wasn't sure yet. But it was enough to make him push harder.

"Mr. Haricharan's death—murder, I should say—is tied to the family's wealth and power. His missing son stands to inherit everything. And yet, you've been running this estate all these years in his absence. I'd imagine... that was hard to accept."

Preetimohan's lips tightened. "Do you have a point, Detective? Or are you just here to stir up old wounds?"

Sen allowed a small smile. "Perhaps both. You see, Mr. Haricharan's will left no room for uncertainty. And yet, here you are, the man in charge. The man who has everything to lose if the rightful heir returns."

Preetimohan's expression remained impassive, but his fingers began to fidget with his cufflinks again, twisting them ever so slightly. Sen's eyes dropped to the small pieces of gold, noting something odd—the initials "H.R." were engraved on them.

"Those are interesting," Sen said casually, gesturing to the cufflinks. "Were they Mr. Haricharan's?"

Preetimohan's hand froze. "A gift," he replied, his voice cool. "From Haricharan. He liked to remind me who was in charge."

Sen nodded slowly. "A reminder... or a warning?"

The silence that followed was thick with unspoken words. Preetimohan didn't answer, and Sen didn't push further—for now.

Mr. Preetimohan folded his hands, and bid Sen farewell. He mumbled something under his breath. It was inaudible to Sen. In his notebook, Sen ticked off the second name- Mrs. Hemlata Raychaudhuri.

The room felt even colder as Mrs. Hemlata Raychaudhuri entered. Her small frame, draped in a pale red sari, moved slowly, each step deliberate and cautious. Her hair, now white, was neatly tied back, but her face bore the weight of the years and grief. She lowered herself into the chair across from Sen with a sigh that seemed to carry the heaviness of a lifetime.

Sen watched her closely, noting the way her hands trembled slightly as they rested in her lap. She looked up at him, her eyes magnified by thick glasses, and offered a weak smile.

"Mrs. Raychaudhuri," Sen began, his voice gentle but probing. "Your family has endured a great deal. First, your grand-daughter, then your son's wife, and now Mr. Haricharan. How are you holding up?"

Her smile faded. "We do what we must to survive, Detective. But there are no words for the kind of pain a mother feels when she loses her children."

Sen nodded sympathetically but didn't let her emotional tone distract him. "It must be difficult, especially with the estate matters still unresolved. Your grandson is still missing... and your husband, Mr. Preetimohan, has been managing everything in his absence."

Hemlata's eyes flickered, and for a brief moment, Sen thought he saw something—anxiety, perhaps, or hesitation.

"Yes," she replied softly. "My husband has taken on the burden. It has not been easy for him."

Sen leaned forward slightly, his gaze steady. "And yet, the estate is tied to your grandson, not to Mr. Preetimohan. Mr. Haricharan's will ensured that everything would pass to his son. Did that cause... any tension in the family?"

Hemlata's hands tensed in her lap, her fingers twisting the fabric of her sari. "No... no tension. Haricharan did what he thought was right. We've always followed tradition."

Sen raised an eyebrow. "Tradition, perhaps, but your family has lost so much. And Mr. Haricharan... did you agree with his decision? To leave the estate in the hands of a son who's been missing for years?"

Her eyes dropped to the floor. "It was Haricharan's choice. Who are we to question it?"

There was something in her voice—too quick, too rehearsed. Sen decided to press further. "And what about Mr. Ramesh?" Sen asked. "He told me Mr. Haricharan mentioned him in the will as well. If his son never returns, Mr. Ramesh stands to inherit everything."

Hemlata's eyes flickered briefly before she looked away. "Haricharan... was a fair man. He didn't want the family's legacy to be left with nothing if his son never came back. Ramesh was always good to him, so Haricharan made sure there was... a contingency."

"You were close to Mr. Haricharan, weren't you? You must have had an opinion about his will. After all, it's not often that a mother has no say in such matters."

Hemlata's eyes shot up, wide and defensive. "Haricharan was... he was a stubborn man. But he was my son. What he did... it was for the family."

Sen caught the slight tremble in her voice and leaned back, his expression calm but his mind racing. "And now, with Mr. Haricharan gone, who do you think should inherit the estate? Surely you or your husband have thought about that."

Hemlata swallowed hard, her fingers still fidgeting. "I don't know, Detective. These things... they are not for me to decide."

Sen glanced at her hands, noticing the way they twisted the fabric of her sari. He'd seen people fidget when they were nervous, but this was different—more like she was trying to hold something back.

"You wear a beautiful ring, Mrs. Raychaudhuri," Sen said suddenly, his tone casual. "May I ask where it's from?"

Her hand froze over the golden band on her finger, a small but ornate piece of jewellery. "This?" she asked, her voice trembling. "It was a gift from Haricharan. A long time ago."

Sen's eyes narrowed slightly, but he kept his tone light. "It's inscribed, isn't it? May I see it?"

For a brief moment, Mrs. Hemlata hesitated, her eyes flicking to the ring and then back to Sen. Slowly, she slid the ring off her finger and handed it to him. Sen turned it over in his hand, examining the small engraving inside: **H.R.**

"It's lovely," he said softly, handing it back to her. "H.R. for Haricharan Raychaudhuri, I assume?"

Hemlata nodded quickly, sliding the ring back onto her finger. "Yes. He gave it to me years ago. It's... a reminder."

"A reminder of what, exactly?"

Hemlata's gaze dropped again, her voice barely a whisper. "That we all have our place in this family, Detective. Haricharan knew his."

Sen allowed the silence to stretch, watching as Mrs. Hemlata's hands resumed their nervous twisting. She was holding something back—he could feel it— but he wasn't ready to push too hard. Not yet.

"Thank you, Mrs. Raychaudhuri," Sen said gently, rising from his seat. "You've been very helpful."

She looked up at him, her eyes filled with something—fear, maybe, or guilt. "You... you will find who did this, won't you?"

Sen paused at the door, turning back to her. "I will. But sometimes, the truth is closer than we think."

As he walked out of the room, Sen couldn't shake the feeling that Mrs. Hemlata was hiding more than just her grief.

The air in the room became thick with passions of malice and secrets as Ramesh Raychaudhuri stepped up next. Sen ticked off the third name.

"Thank you for meeting with me, Mr. Ramesh," Sen began, his voice steady and calm. "I know this is a difficult time for your family."

Ramesh nodded; his throat dry. "I just want to find out who killed Haricharan. He was my cousin, and now... now he's gone."

Sen leaned forward slightly; his expression serious. "Let's start with the night of his death. Where were you?"

"I was in my room," Ramesh replied, his voice trembling. "I heard some noises, but I thought it was just the wind. I didn't think anything of it."

"Did you see anyone else in the house that night?" Sen pressed, his eyes narrowing. "Anyone who might have had a motive?"

Ramesh hesitated, his hands fidgeting. "No, I didn't see anyone. Everyone was asleep, or at least I thought they were."

Sen studied him closely. "You mentioned hearing noises. Can you describe them? Did they sound like a struggle?"

Ramesh's gaze dropped to the floor. "I... I don't know. It was dark, and I was half-asleep. I didn't think it was anything serious."

"Yet you were aware enough to hear something," Sen noted, his tone probing. "What about the marigolds? They seem to be a common thread in these murders. Did you notice anything unusual about them?"

Ramesh's eyes widened, and he shook his head vigorously. "No! I didn't pay much attention to the garden. It's just a garden, isn't it?"

Sen leaned back, considering Ramesh's words. "A garden that has become a source of multiple crimes. You must understand the significance. Did Mr. Haricharan ever express fear about the marigolds or anyone in the family?"

Ramesh shifted in his seat; his discomfort palpable. "He mentioned feeling watched… but I thought he was just stressed about the estate and the family issues."

"Family issues?" Sen raised an eyebrow. "Can you elaborate? Rivalries? Disputes?"

"There have always been tensions," Ramesh admitted, his voice barely above a whisper. "Especially with the property. Haricharan was worried about the will. He thought someone might want to take it from him."

Sen's expression hardened. "And what about you, Mr. Ramesh? You are also a potential heir to Haricharan's estate, are you not?"

Ramesh's defensiveness flared. "Of course! But I have no claim to anything here. I'm just a cousin."

"Yet, if Mr. Haricharan's son remains missing, you stand to inherit everything," Sen pointed out, his tone sharp. "How do I know you didn't want to eliminate Mr. Haricharan for your own benefit?"

"That's absurd!" Ramesh exclaimed, his voice rising. "I loved him like a brother! Why would I do that?"

Sen's gaze remained unwavering. "Love can sometimes lead to jealousy, especially in families with a history like yours. You must understand, I need to explore every possibility." Ramesh's shoulders slumped, and he looked defeated. "I swear, I didn't harm him! I just want to find out who did this!"

"Then help me, Mr. Ramesh. Who else was in the house that night? Anyone who might have had a motive?" Sen pressed, his voice softening slightly.

Ramesh hesitated, his eyes flickering with uncertainty. "There was... there was a stranger I saw lurking in the garden a few days before. I didn't think much of it then."

"A stranger?" Sen's interest piqued. "What did he look like?"

"He was tall, wearing a dark coat... I thought he was just a passerby," Ramesh replied, his voice trembling.

Sen noted the change in Ramesh's demeanour. "And you didn't think to mention this earlier? This could be crucial information."

"I didn't think it was important at the time," Ramesh said, his voice barcly above a whisper. Sen leaned back in his chair, contemplating the young man before him. "Mr. Ramesh, your family has been through a lot. But secrets have a way of coming to light. If you know anything else, now is the time to share it." Ramesh looked up, his eyes filled with a mix of fear and desperation. "I just want to find out who did this. I can't bear the thought of losing anyone else."

"Very well," Sen said, rising from his seat. "I'll need to speak with Mr. Amit Patel as well. We must piece together the events leading up to Haricharan's death."

As Sen nodded, relief mingled with anxiety on his face, Ramesh walked out of the room, the weight of his secrets lingering in the air. He couldn't shake the feeling that the young man was hiding something—something that could hold the key to unravelling the mystery of the Raychaudhuri family's tragic fate.

The atmosphere in the room was heavy. Sen's mind spoke unspoken volumes. Mr. Amit Patel, secretary of the late, Mr. Haricharan Raychaudhuri took a seat. Sen ticked off the fourth, and the final name.

"Mr. Patel," Sen said, addressing him directly. "Thank you for being here. I need to ask you a few questions regarding Haricharan's death and the events leading up to it."

Amit nodded; his expression serious. "I'll do my best to help, Detective."

Sen leaned, observing the slight tremor in Amit's hands as they rested on his lap. "Let's start with your relationship with Mr. Haricharan. How long have you worked for him?"

"About six years," Amit replied, his voice steady but laced with an undercurrent of tension. "I was his secretary and confidant. He trusted me with many matters concerning the estate."

"Trust is a fragile thing, especially in a family with so much at stake," Sen noted. "What can you tell me about the threats Mr. Haricharan received? Did he confide in you about any specific concerns?"

Amit hesitated, glancing at the clock before responding. "He mentioned feeling uneasy, especially after the murders of his wife and daughter. He believed someone was watching him, but he didn't share the details of the threats with me until recently."

Sen raised his eyebrow, sensing the weight of Amit's words. "And what about the will? Mr. Haricharan had made it clear that his estate would pass to his missing son. How did that affect the family dynamics?"

Amit's brow furrowed. "There was tension, especially with Ramesh. He felt entitled to a share of the estate, considering he was the only other male heir present. Haricharan's decision to leave everything to his son created a rift."

"Interesting," Sen replied, his mind racing with possibilities. "Did you ever witness any arguments between Mr. Ramesh and Mr. Haricharan regarding the will?"

Amit shifted uncomfortably in his seat. "There were heated discussions, yes. Ramesh was frustrated by the situation, but I never thought it had a chance to escalate to violence."

Sen studied Amit's demeanour closely. "You mentioned that Mr. Haricharan trusted you. Did he ever express fear for his life?"

"Yes," Amit admitted, his voice barely above a whisper. "He was terrified. He believed someone was out to get him, and he feared he would be next."

"Did he ever mention anyone specific?" Sen pressed, his eyes narrowing.

Amit hesitated again, his gaze flicking to the window. "He mentioned family rivals, but he didn't name anyone directly. He seemed to think it was someone close to him."

Sen leaned back, contemplating Amit's words. "And what about you, Mr. Patel? Where were you on the night of Mr. Haricharan's murder?"

"I was here only," Amit replied quickly. "I received a call from him earlier that evening about some estate matters, but I didn't think much of it at the time."

"Did you hear anything unusual? Any sounds or disturbances coming from the estate?" Sen asked, his tone probing.

Amit shook his head. "No, nothing. It was a quiet night."

Sen's expression hardened. "You understand that your position as his secretary puts you in a unique position, don't you? You had access to him and the estate. That makes you a person of interest."

Amit's eyes widened, panic flaring. "Detective, I would never harm Haricharan! He was like a father to me. I just want to see justice served for him and the family."

"Then you shall also have to help me, Mr. Amit," Sen urged, his voice steady. "If you know anything else, anything at all, now is the time to share it. Secrets have a way of coming to light, and it's better if you're the one to reveal them."

Amit took a deep breath, his hands clenching into fists. "I swear, I didn't know anything about the marigolds or the cyanide until after the police arrived. I was just as shocked as everyone else."

"Very well," Sen said, rising from his seat. "I'll need to speak with the others as well. But remember, your cooperation is crucial. If you have more information, it could help clear your name."

Patel walked out of the room, the weight of the conversation lingering in the air. He couldn't overlook the feeling that Amit Patel was holding back—perhaps out of fear or loyalty—and that the truth about Haricharan's death was still shrouded in secrecy.

Chapter 21

SENIOR ADVOCATE RAKESH BHUIYAN

Sen met Prasad later in the evening. Prasad hurriedly came and asked Sen, "How did it go?"

"It was fine. I could recover many clues. There is some stranger roaming around the estate. Mr. Ramesh told me this. Then, Mr. Preetimohan and Mrs. Hemlata appeared to be normal. I do not know why but Mr. Preetimohan appears a little too calm."

Prasad raised his brow, and said, "Maybe cause he's mentally strong".

Sen strongly nodded in disapproval. "Everything is fishy, Prasad. Have you got the appointment to Mr. Rakesh?"

"Oh! Yes! I have. I have scheduled it at 8p.m."

8'o clock in the night came, and Sen found themselves at Rakesh Bhuiyan, Senior Advocate, Lawyer of the late Haricharan.

The law office of Senior Advocate Rakesh Bhuiyan was as imposing as its reputation. Dark wooden panels lined the walls, and the air was thick with the scent of old leather and polished brass. Sen sat across from Bhuiyan, who was meticulously organizing a stack of papers on his desk.

Bhuiyan finally looked up, his eyes sharp behind rimless glasses. "Detective Sen, I presume? How can I assist you?"

Sen leaned back slightly, studying the man. "Mr. Bhuiyan, you were Haricharan Raychaudhuri's lawyer. I need to understand the exact details of his will."

Bhuiyan nodded, a slight frown creasing his forehead. "Of course. Haricharan's will was straightforward. The estate is to be inherited by his son, should he ever return. If not, it passes to his cousin, Ramesh."

Sen's eyes narrowed. "Was there anything unusual about the will? Any recent changes or additions?"

Bhuiyan hesitated, his fingers tapping lightly on the desk. "Haricharan did make a change shortly before his death. He was... concerned about the will. He added a clause that if neither his son nor Ramesh could inherit, the estate would be sold and the proceeds donated to charity."

Sen's eyebrows raised in surprise. "That's quite a drastic measure. Did he say why?"

Bhuiyan sighed, removing his glasses and rubbing the bridge of his nose. "He seemed paranoid. He talked about threats and felt that the estate might become a curse if left within the family. He was deeply troubled, Detective."

Sen leaned forward, his tone probing. "Were there any specific threats he mentioned? Any names?"

Bhuiyan shook his head. "No names. Just a general sense of impending doom. He was particularly worried about the marigolds. He believed they were an omen."

Sen's mind raced, connecting the dots. "Mr. Bhuiyan, I've noticed that everyone involved seems to have their secrets. Tell me, do you believe Ramesh could have had a motive to kill Haricharan?"

Bhuiyan paused, a calculated look crossing his face. "Ramesh was always loyal to Haricharan. But loyalty can be a fickle thing when wealth and power are involved. I suppose it's possible, but I have no evidence to support such a claim."

Sen nodded slowly. "What about you, Mr. Bhuiyan? Did you benefit in any way from Haricharan's death?"

Bhuiyan's eyes flashed with irritation. "Detective, I am a man of the law. My duty is to my clients, and I assure you, I had no reason to wish harm upon Haricharan. My only concern was to carry out his wishes as he stipulated in his will."

Sen's gaze didn't waver. "You were the last person to see him alive, weren't you? The night before he died, he came to you."

Bhuiyan's composure faltered slightly. "Yes, he did. He was in a state of distress, more so than I had ever seen him. He spoke about the marigolds, about feeling watched. I tried to calm him, but he left my office in a hurry."

Sen leaned back, contemplating the advocate's words. "One last question, Mr. Bhuiyan. These cryptic letters Haricharan received—do you have any idea who might have sent them?"

Bhuiyan shook his head firmly. "I'm afraid not. Haricharan never showed them to me. He only mentioned them in passing, as part of his growing paranoia."

Sen rose from his chair, extending his hand. "Thank you for your time, Mr. Bhuiyan. You've been very helpful."

Bhuiyan shook Sen's hand, his grip firm but cold. "I hope you find the answers you seek, Detective. Haricharan deserves justice."

As Sen walked out of the office, his mind was filled with more questions than answers. Bhuiyan had revealed important details, but something about his demeanour didn't sit right. The advocate was hiding something—Sen was sure of it. And he intended to find out what it was.

Chapter 22

WEB OF LIES

All routine investigations were taking place. Five days had gone by. Sen was still in a dilemma, unable to connect the knots. Haricharan was murdered, but why? He had an enemy, Mr. Rakshit, who suffers from Arthritis. It was all very improbable. Who was the mysterious, strong man, that warned Sen to ward off the case? Who was the man seen roaming around the estate on the day of the murder? To whom does the ring inscribed, 'R.R' belong to? There were more questions than answers. Why were Marigolds only chosen? Only a student of Botany would be able to execute such precise cyanide-lacing. Where is Haricharan's son? What had happened to him? Why were Haricharan's daughter and wife also killed? Reasons. Reasons, were all Sen wanted.

Prasad came in to meet Sen, who was in a state of meditation. Prasad whispered, "Sen, Sen. I have something to tell you."

Sen murmured, "Hm."

"Upon closer inspection of the deceased's room, a handkerchief has been found tucked behind the door. Upon forensic search, fingerprints have not been discovered, but traces of cyanide and marigold, have been found."

Sen sighed, and concluded, "That means nothing. It was used by our murderer to carry the cyanide-laced marigold."

Prasad confused, uttered, "What shall we do next then? We are stuck in a loop, it seems."

"We surely are. But I have got some conceptions, only proper to myself."

"Come on Sen! Let them out!"

Sen straightened his back, and ordered a cup of coffee. The coffee came. The entire room was filled with the mesmerizing smell of the finely, refined coffee.

Sen muttered, "Hm! The London One, this."

Prasad now frustrated, almost screamed, "Come to the damned case, Sen."

Sen came back to his senses, and started speaking, "Yes. That. All these evidences point to that one man.

One man only, Prasad. That man also has motives, as far as I know"

"Who?"

Sen smirked, and replied in quick fashion, "Ramesh Raychaudhuri."

Prasad frowned. It was total amazement for him.

Sen let the silence hang for a moment, and then uttered, "First, he is not getting the share after all. Thus, he had also argued with his brother about that. Second, he visits the garden often, which is evident from my discovery."

Sen proudly took out the ring, he had discovered; from a leather case. Prasad was baffled by all of it.

Sen continued, "And then, Mr. Ramesh's stories are too smooth to be believed. But then these are just speculations. Nothing can be assured. But I think we need to make a search of each person's room. I believe we shall find something interesting."

Prasad could only nod. The silence that followed was deafening…

Chapter 23

THE SEARCH

Everything was set for the day. Sen was prepared for a search of the Palashabari estate. Prasad was grim about the matter. A list was prepared of the names. First up was Mr. Preetimohan Raychaudhuri. He did not object to it. Nothing of much importance was found, except a peculiar, broken syringe near the window.

Sen asked, "What is that, Mr. Preetimohan?"

For the first time, Mr. Preetimohan's voice shook a little but he firmly answered after, "That was a wasted syringe for my diabetes."

Sen rapidly fired, "Do you really have diabetes?"

Mr. Preetimohan, still firm in his voice, "And why should I lie about that?"

Sen countered, "You do know that yours is the closest to Mr. Haricharan's room?"

Mr. Preetimohan fidgeted a little, but replied, the same steadiness in his voice, "Detective. You are questioning Hari's father. Be careful whom you blame, and suspect. No father in this world would want to kill their child."

Sen nodded, and went up to Mrs. Hemlata Raychaudhuri's room. Her room was the simplest Sen had seen. There was an idol of Lord Ganesha on the table, which was strewn with garlands and incense sticks. The fresh aroma of the incense sticks filled the room. Nothing was found in the room except a garland of Marigolds kept on the table. Sen pointed at them and asked, "What might be those?"

"Th-those are for Ganesha's puja. Not for that you are thinking!"

Sen sighed, and proceeded to Amit Patel's room. His room was simple as well. However, the simplest things hold the darkest secrets. There were curtains drawn over windows, and a freshly, dusted typewriter kept on the bookshelf with a pile of paper beside it. There were a lot of books arranged on the shelf, and a few pens kept on the table.

A bunch of letters, a half-burnt piece of paper, and an enigmatic photograph was discovered.

Sen fixed his sleeves, and asked, "Why were these letters hidden inside your mattress?"

Patel hesitated, and spoke, "Mr. Haricharan had told me to keep these letters hidden from his family members. He was running in debt as well. All these letters are about that."

Sen raised his brow, and uttered, "He had told so, or do you have any personal reason? Anyways, what about this half-burnt piece of paper?"

Patel swallowed air, spoke hastily, "That was a letter of threat for Mr. Haricharan. He had told me to burn that specific letter, because he could not take them anymore."

Sen smirked, and spoke, "Your words make a good story. What do you have for the photograph?"

Patel looked at the clock, and uttered, "That was Mr. Haricharan's family picture."

Sen ended his session with a quick glance into Patel's eyes. Fear had completely smeared over Patel. Sen walked up to the last room of inquiry- Ramesh Raychaudhuri's room. His room was just as simple as Mrs. Hemlata's was. Ramesh was sitting on his chair, near the window. His gaze fixed upon the marigold garden. Sen coughed, and broke the uncanny silence. Ramesh switched his look towards Sen. He asked, "How may I help you again?"

Sen answered, steadily, "We have to do a search of your room."

Ramesh answered politely, "Surely you can."

There was a hint of anxiety in his tone. Sen did not pay heed to it, and instructed Prasad to carry on with the search.

Sen looked at Ramesh, who was unmoved. Sen smirked, and uttered, "You do often visit the garden, don't you?"

Ramesh moved a little in his chair, and answered, "W-What do you mean?"

Seb answered, still firm, "You know very well what I mean? I had found your ring that day, with 'R.R.' inscribed onto it."

Ramesh completely fell silent. Sen continued, "Why? May I know the reason?"

Ramesh, fidgeted his hands, and replied, with a shaky voice, "I-It is not what it looks like. I-I can explain. My mother had told me to fetch some marigolds from the garden, and for that…"

Sen countered, "Good enough. Prasad did you find anything?"

Prasad heftily, lifted a heavy book, and shoved it into Sen's hands. "Found this book of Botany."

Sen smiled, and looked at Ramesh, his brow raised. "What's this Mr. Ramesh?"

Ramesh again dropped into silence. He gulped down air, and answered, "T-That book is of my father. He was a graduate in Botany. So, he had forced me to study the same."

Sen nodded, and finally said, "Then, Mr. Ramesh, I hope you do know what that means."

With that, Sen walked out of the room with Prasad. Ramesh was left swirling in his chair. The same words were repeating over and over in his mind, "I didn't kill him. I didn't kill him or anyone… I really didn't…"

Chapter 24

SEN SITS BACK AND THINKS

The routine search and enquiry were done with. A lot of new information laid with Sen. Now it was time to piece them together. Prasad accompanied Sen to his house. They went up the stairs, and got themselves seated in Sen's room. Sen threw off his coat on the couch, and sat on his easy-chair. He closed his eyes. The silence was horrific. Eventually Prasad opened his mouth, "Sen. Sen. Know whodunnit?"

Sen calmly shook his head. "Negative.", he replied.

Prasad asked, with irritation ringing in his voice, "How much more? How long? At the brink, and still no solution."

Sen still composed, replied, "I was running in a completely wrong direction. Today, I have opened my eyes. The entire case has turned upside-down. What I now think, is something much terrible. But I fear it might be true."

Prasad flinched, and said, "But then who? You know its Ramesh; I know its Ramesh. We have the proof against him. Then how can he not be?"

Sen smiled, and replied, "Dear Prasad. There is more to what meets the eye. What if the proofs are set up to trap Mr. Ramesh. Think. Think. My solution will appear too bizarre to your programmed brain."

Prasad gave up, and flung his hands. "Fine you win."

Sen now sat up. He looked at Sen. His eyes had that glimmer. He picked up the photograph he had collected today. He asked Prasad, "Do you know why I picked up this photograph today?"

Prasad smiled, and said, "No why?"

Sen smirked, and answered firmly, "If you see with my eyes, there is something missing in this picture."

Prasad joked, "But then I do not have 'your eyes'! So kindly reveal!"

Sen didn't smile. His mood became grave all of a sudden. He said, "In this picture, there is young Haricharan, his father, his mother, Mr. Amit Patel, Prafulla babu but the fun lies here. Mr. Ramesh Raychaudhuri is not present in this picture."

Prasad was shocked. He stammered, "B-But h-how can that be? He must be…"

Sen replied without hesitation, "Because he hasn't yet been born into this family."

Chapter 25

SURPRISING REVELATIONS

The silence that followed was petrifying! No words were spoken, but Sen's words had done the magic. Prasad felt at a loss of words. Finally, he said, "Sen. That looks grave. That means Ramesh is not the cousin of Haricharan."

Sen nodded, and answered, "Precisely so. Not Mr. Haricharan's cousin but his son. Mr. Ramesh Raychaudhuri is Mr. Haricharan's long-lost son. The reason for Mr. Haricharan having addressed him as cousin would be better from the horse's mouth. Let us see."

Prasad nodded in approval, and uttered, "I knew that fellow was a scoundrel. But then who murdered Haricharan?"

Sen chuckled, and replied, "Isn't it very obvious 'whodunnit'?"

With that Sen rose and donned his coat. Prasad was still in confusion but still caught up with Sen. Both of them got into Sen's car, and drifted off towards Palashbari estate. It was time for some more fun…

Sen swept inside the room of Mr. Preetimohan like a hurricane. Mr. Preetimohan was resting on his chair, eyes closed. Sen flapped his hand on the table. Mr. Preetimohan opened his eyes, and wore his glasses. He looked straight into Sen's eyes, and asked, "Mr. Ramesh was never your son. Nor was he the cousin of Mr. Haricharan. He was the damned son of Mr. Haricharan."

Mr. Preetimohan answered, unmoved, "So you finally found out. Yes. 'Tis true."

Sen spat out his words, "You knew this all along, didn't you?"

Mr. Preetimohan nodded, and firmly replied, "Hari always knew his son's alibi. Then after several years when his son is at least 25 years old, he brings him in, and disguises his own son as his cousin. He forced everyone to believe it. And even me."

Sen understood the gravity of the situation. He replied sensibly, "Mr. Preetimohan, I would like to meet Prafulla Babu once."

Mr. Preetimohan called Prafulla Ghosh and informed him about Sen's wish. Prafulla agreed, and waited outside. Sen bid farewell to Mr. Preetimohan. He met Prafulla outside. Prafulla rose and greeted both Sen and Prasad. Sen started, "You were there present in the house on the night of Mr. Haricharan's murder?"

Prafulla replied, "Yes Babu."

Sen continued with approval, watching Prafulla's every move with a hawk's gaze, "On the night of Haricharan's death. You had seen more that you're letting on."

Prafulla's hands twitched at his sides, but he said nothing, his eyes fixed on the floor.

"Answer me, Prafulla Babu," Sen pressed, his tone sharper now. "You've been working in this family for years. You know its secrets. You were in the house that night. What did you see?"

Prafulla's throat moved as he swallowed hard, but still, he didn't speak. The tension in the room grew thicker.

"I don't have time for games," Sen said, his voice low, dangerous. "If you're hiding something, you'd better speak up now, before it's too late."

Finally, Prafulla looked up, his eyes meeting Sen's for the first time since the conversation started. "Babu... I didn't kill him," he whispered, his voice shaking. "I swear on everything, I didn't."

Sen remained silent, waiting.

"I—I was just there, in the hallway," Prafulla stammered, his voice trembling as he recalled the events. "I heard voices. Haricharan babu was speaking to someone... I don't know who."

Sen's eyes narrowed. "What did you hear?"

Prafulla's breathing quickened, and he wiped the sweat forming on his brow. "I couldn't make out all the words... but they were arguing. Haricharan sounded angry, and then there was... silence."

"And then what happened?"

Prafulla's hands trembled as he clasped them together. "I didn't want to interfere. I stayed hidden. But when I went back later, he was already lying there, cold. The marigold was in his hand."

Sen leaned forward. "And who was the person he was arguing with, Prafulla Babu? You know, don't you?"

Prafulla shook his head frantically, but his eyes darted to the side, betraying his fear. Sen caught the movement and pressed harder. "Tell me the truth. Was it Mr. Ramesh?"

Prafulla's lips quivered, and for a moment, it looked as though he might break. But he said nothing.

Sen's patience was wearing thin. He stood up abruptly, towering over Prafulla. "You're protecting someone. I can see it in your eyes. But you can't keep quiet forever, Prafulla. The truth will come out, and when it does, you'll regret not speaking sooner."

Prafulla's head dropped, his shoulders sagging with the weight of his guilt. "I... I don't know anything for sure, Babu," he muttered. "But Ramesh Babu... he had been acting strange. He was always lurking around that night, near Haricharan babu's room."

Sen's gaze sharpened. "And what did you see him do?"

Prafulla hesitated again, his voice barely a whisper. "I saw him leave the room... just before I found Haricharan Babu."

Sen's eyes flashed with realization, but he kept his expression unreadable. "Thank you, Prafulla Babu," he said quietly. "You've been very helpful."

Without another word, Prafulla shuffled out of Sen's sight, his steps heavy with the burden of his confession. Sen stood alone, his mind racing with the implications of what he'd just heard.

Prasad asked, "Sen, what do you make of this?"

Sen, confidently spoke, "Prasad. We have to question Mr. Ramesh for one last time."

Prasad joked, "To confirm he is the killer?"

Sen paid no heed, and uttered, "Open your eyes, Prasad."

The air was thick with tension as Sen stood before Ramesh, who sat hunched in the chair, eyes downcast. The dim light cast long shadows, and for a moment, the silence in the room seemed unbearable.

"You've been lying, Mr. Ramesh," Sen said quietly, his voice like a cold blade cutting through the room. "About who you really are."

Ramesh's head snapped up; his eyes wide with shock. "I haven't—"

"Enough," Sen interrupted, his tone firm. "You are not Mr. Haricharan's cousin. You're his son."

The words hung in the air, and for a moment, it seemed as though time had stopped. Ramesh's face drained of colour, his mouth opening but no sound escaping.

Ramesh slumped in the chair, his breath shallow, his face pale. Sen's words had struck a nerve, but Ramesh remained silent, his eyes darting around the room.

"Mr. Ramesh, you've been hiding something," Sen said, his voice firm but measured. "You're Mr. Haricharan's son. But you didn't claim your place in the family, did you?"

Ramesh's eyes flickered, but he still said nothing. The tension in the room grew heavier.

"You were meant to inherit everything," Sen continued. "But you let Mr. Preetimohan handle the estate. Why?"

Ramesh's shoulders sagged further, his hands trembling slightly. "I didn't want it... I didn't want any of this," he whispered.

Sen narrowed his eyes. "What do you mean by that?"

Ramesh's voice faltered as he spoke. "My grandfather... he... he always said it was for the best. That I wasn't ready. He promised he'd... take care of things until I was ready."

Sen leaned forward. "So, you trusted him?"

Ramesh hesitated. "I... I didn't question him. He was family... I thought he had my best interests at heart. But now... now I'm not so sure."

Sen's gaze hardened. "Not so sure? Why, Mr. Ramesh? What changed?"

Ramesh swallowed, his voice barely above a whisper. "After Father's death, I started to wonder... but I have no proof."

The session was done with. Sen walked out of the estate with Prasad, his head held high. It felt Sen had cracked the case. He only needed a few proofs to set it on line...

When they had got in the car again, Prasad asked, "Where to next?"

Sen answered, with a firm grip on his tone, "Senior Advocate Rakesh Bhuiyan."

Both of them reached the desired place. The same old law office. The atmosphere was somber as usual. The office was quiet, except for the faint ticking of the old clock on the wall. Advocate Rakesh Bhuiyan sat behind his desk, his fingers absentmindedly tapping a stack of papers. Sen could tell he was holding something back.

"There's something you haven't told me, Mr. Bhuiyan," Sen began, breaking the silence. "Haricharan's will—it wasn't complete, was it?"

Bhuiyan's hand stilled, and he sighed deeply. "No, Detective, it wasn't."

Sen leaned forward; his gaze sharp. "Why wasn't it completed? What was he planning to change?"

Bhuiyan adjusted his glasses, hesitating. "Haricharan was worried, more so than I'd ever seen him. He feared something was coming, though he never specified what. He wanted to add a clause—something about what would happen in the event of his 'untimely' or... 'enigmatic' death. But he never got the chance to finish it."

Sen's eyes narrowed. "Why not?"

Bhuiyan shook his head. "He didn't trust anyone, not even me, towards the end. He started drafting it on his own, but... well, whatever he planned to add is lost with him."

Sen smiled, and thanked Mr. Rakesh a thousand times. After leaving Mr. Bhuiyan's office, Sen's mind buzzed with lingering doubts. There was one final detail needed to be verified before the confrontation. He veered off to Mr. Preetimohan, one last time, and obtained the name of the university from where Mr. Preetimohan had passed out. The year of graduation was also noted. The call was made to the university registrar, where the officials confirmed, "Yes, Mr. Preetimohan was a graduate of our university. Yes, indeed. In Botany."

Done. Sen hung up the call, and smiled even more. The final piece of the puzzle had been found…

Chapter 26

CHALKING OUT THE MOTIVES

Prasad was waiting for Sen at the latter's house. Sen swept in like a hurricane, and took a seat. Excitement burning down in every step. Prasad asked, with a hint of sarcasm, "Done, is it?"

Sen replied, confidently, "Yes. The puzzle is complete. Now I lay down the motives in front of you. Then guess 'whodunnit'?"

Prasad nodded in approval, and asked Sen to continue. Sen, having got an opportunity began, "First let us come to Mrs. Hemlata Raychaudhuri. Yes, she might have some motives to kill her son, but she did not have enough courage. She just couldn't dare to lay a finger on her own son.

Next let us arrive to Mr. Amit Patel. Well, he did not have any such motive to kill Mr. Haricharan. But he is involved in this affair. How? I shall reveal it tomorrow when I confront the killer.

Then comes our Prafulla Babu. He could not have killed Mr. Haricharan. But yes, he is guarding an individual. A certain individual."

There was a slight pause. Prasad shifted a little in his chair. Sen continued, "Mr. Ramesh Raychaudhuri is the one with the best motive. As the son, and heir to Mr. Haricharan's property, he could've had the motive to remove his father once and for all. The way his father and grandfather kept his identity hidden, also adds a layer of spice. But why kill his mother and sister too?

Next in line, is our Mr. Harshit Shyamlal. The businessman, and owner of Shyamlal & Sons. But I strongly believe he had no ulterior motive.

Then, Mr. Rakshit Kumar. Although, he hated Mr. Haricharan from the core. His arthritis disabled him to do anything. Thus, we can count both businessmen out of our list.

Finally comes Mr. Preetimohan. Surprisingly I found out, that even he had the greatest motive to kill Mr. Haricharan. He wanted to establish his power over the estate, but Mr. Haricharan did not want so. He was old, but he had an ardent desire to control the empire in his last moments. So, it be. Mr. Preetimohan decided to remove the thorn from the rose once and for all. And, now Prasad, what do you think? Whodunnit?"

Prasad's eye flickered, "I still believe its Ramesh. Even you are saying so."

Sen, his patience wearing thin, snapped with irritation in his voice, "Prasad. My dear Prasad. Are you really still convinced it's Mr. Ramesh? Use your brain. He was nothing more than a carefully executed scapegoat."

Prasad frowned, his gaze a mix of confusion and amazement. His voice trembled as he stuttered, "T-Then... who is it? If it's not Ramesh, WHO IS IT?"

Sen's voice steadied, becoming grave. "It may be hard to believe... but the real culprit is... Mr. Preetimohan."

Prasad's eyes widened, his breath catching in his throat. "Mr. Preetimohan? But... why? Why would he—"

Sen cut him off, his voice steady but charged with intensity. "It's simple, Prasad. He was never meant to inherit the estate, not while Mr. Haricharan's son, Mr. Ramesh, was alive. The will, unfinished as it was, still placed Ramesh as the rightful heir. Mr. Preetimohan had everything to gain—and he knew that."

Prasad shook his head, still struggling to process the information. "But how could he—"

Sen's eyes gleamed with cold clarity. "The marigolds, Prasad. Mr. Preetimohan had knowledge of botany—far more than he let on. He used that knowledge to his advantage. Cyanide, extracted from the very flowers Haricharan loved, was his weapon. He was counting on us to overlook him; to assume he was just another grieving relative."

Prasad's expression twisted with disbelief. "But Ramesh was his scapegoat all along?"

Sen nodded, his voice firm. "Mr. Preetimohan manipulated everyone. He planted the seeds of doubt around Ramesh, knowing full well that once we looked closely, Ramesh would seem like the perfect suspect. A man hidden in plain sight, yet guilty of nothing but being the son, Mr. Haricharan tried to protect."

Prasad stood, pacing now, frustration etched across his face. "So, it was all about the inheritance?"

Sen's tone turned grave. "Yes. Mr. Preetimohan stood to gain control over the entire estate, especially once the will remained unfinished. Mr. Haricharan's growing paranoia—his fear of an 'untimely death'— gave Mr. Mr. Haricharan could finalize the will. The marigolds were his signature... his mark of control."

Prasad stopped in his tracks. "And the cryptic letters?"

Sen's eyes narrowed; his voice now cold as ice. "Mr. Preetimohan sent them, not himself, but through somebody. And, I do know that 'somebody'! They were designed to push Mr. Haricharan over the edge, feeding his paranoia, making him believe someone was after him. All while Mr. Preetimohan was right there—acting the part of a concerned family member."

A heavy silence filled the room as Prasad slumped back into his chair, overwhelmed by the truth. Sen, however, remained focused, his mind already turning to the final confrontation.

"There's only one thing left to do," Sen said quietly, standing to leave. "We confront him."

Chapter 27

AND THEN THERE IS THE TRUTH…

The room was dimly lit, casting long shadows on the walls as Sen entered, his every step echoing ominously against the polished floor. Mr. Preetimohan sat at the end of the large table, his hands folded calmly in front of him. His expression was unreadable—calm, even—but Sen could see the flicker of anxiety in his eyes.

Sen's voice cut through the silence. "It's over, Mr. Preetimohan. I know everything."

Mr. Preetimohan remained still, his face betraying no emotion. "I'm afraid I don't know what you mean, Detective," he said coolly. "Everything?"

Sen's eyes narrowed. "The marigolds. The cyanide. The letters. It all points back to you."

A faint smile touched Mr. Preetimohan's lips. "You're mistaken."

But Sen was relentless. "You used Ramesh as a pawn. A convenient scapegoat, wasn't he? All while you sat back and watched the chaos unfold. You sent those letters, you fed Mr. Haricharan's fears, and when the moment was right, you struck."

Mr. Preetimohan's smile faltered ever so slightly. "You have no proof."

Sen stepped forward, unflinching. "You thought you could play everyone. You manipulated Mr. Haricharan's paranoia, poisoned him with cyanide from the marigolds, and tried to use Mr. Ramesh as a scapegoat."

Mr. Preetimohan remained quiet, but his fingers twitched.

"And it wasn't just you," Sen continued, his eyes narrowing. "You had help, didn't you? Mr. Amit Patel—he sent the threats. He wrote the letters that pushed Mr. Haricharan over the edge. But it wasn't his plan. It was yours."

Mr. Preetimohan's calm expression finally cracked. His eyes flickered with a mixture of anger and fear.

Sen pressed on. "Mr. Amit Patel may have delivered the letters, but you controlled everything. You fed him the lies, had him play the part of the anonymous threat to make Haricharan paranoid. You preyed on

Mr. Haricharan's growing fears, using Mr. Amit as your tool."

Mr. Preetimohan's voice was barely a whisper. "Amit... was a fool. Easy to manipulate. He believed everything I told him."

Sen stepped closer; his voice sharp. "And while Amit played his part, you took care of the rest. You killed Haricharan's wife and daughter—both of them stood in the way of your plans for the estate. And when Haricharan started to catch on, you knew it was time to eliminate him too. You murdered his wife. She was the first obstacle. She would have protected the estate after Mr. Haricharan's death, made sure Mr. Ramesh received his rightful inheritance. So, you had to get rid of her. It was the only way to secure your control. And then his daughter," Sen continued, his voice growing colder. "She was next in line after Mr. Haricharan. If she inherited the estate, everything would have fallen apart for you. So, you killed her too. A tragic accident, they said. But it was no accident, was it, Mr. Preetimohan?"

The room was silent, the tension palpable as Mr. Preetimohan's fingers twitched again.

"You orchestrated their deaths," Sen pressed, his eyes narrowing. "And when Mr. Haricharan finally realized what was happening, you knew your time was running out. He was going to change the will—add a clause to protect his estate from falling into your hands."

Mr. Preetimohan's voice was quiet but seething. "You think you're so clever, don't you?"

"You think you're clever, don't you?" Sen continued. "But you made a mistake. You claimed to have no knowledge of botany, but I checked. You're not only familiar with plants, Mr. Preetimohan—you specialized in them. And who else but a botanist would know how to extract cyanide from marigolds?"

Mr. Preetimohan's face hardened, his calm exterior cracking as his eyes flashed with something darker. "You think you've outsmarted me, Detective? Do you know what it's like to watch everything slip through your fingers, to have your life's work handed to a fool?"

Sen stepped closer, his voice colder now. "I know what it's like to see someone twist a family's legacy for their own gain. But it's over. You won't escape this."

Mr. Preetimohan rose to his feet, his composure shattering as he glared at Sen. "I did what was necessary! Haricharan was weak—too soft to lead this family! Ramesh was no better. Someone had to protect the legacy!"

"And for that, you killed him," Sen replied sharply. "You poisoned him, made it look like a tragedy, and framed his own son."

Mr. Preetimohan's breathing quickened, his eyes wild with desperation. "You have no idea what it was like! I kept this family together. Without me, everything would have fallen apart!"

Sen's voice was cold, final. "You did not save the family, you destroyed it. And now you'll answer for it."

The door behind them opened, and Prasad stepped into the room, followed by two officers. Mr. Preetimohan's face drained of colour as he realized there was no way out.

"You've made your last move, Mr. Preetimohan," Sen said quietly, nodding to the officers.

As they approached to arrest him, Mr. Preetimohan's shoulders sagged in defeat, the weight of his actions finally crashing down on him. His once calm and calculated demeanour were gone, replaced by a hollow shell of a man who had gambled everything—and lost.

Chapter 28

AFTER THE STORM...

A week had gone by, after the 'Marigold Case'. Prasad now resided with Sen, aiming to be an accomplice.

Sen joked, "So, you have decided to act as my Watson?"

Prasad laughed, and answered, "Precisely so. But Sen I still have one doubt. How could you understand that it was that scoundrel Preetimohan, and not Ramesh."

Sen heaved a sigh of confusion, and replied, "It was all so set-up. It felt too easy for me. All evidences led to that one man. But could it be so easy? Then I started thinking complex. And, the idea of Mr. Preetimohan clicked to me. Why? He wanted control over the empire he had created with his own hands.

So, he deserved to get a chance to rule it for one last time… So…"

Prasad applauded Sen. It was yet another feather on Sen's cap…

The End